I0771446

Gnashing Teeth Publishing
242 East Main Street
Norman AR 71960
http://GnashingTeethPublishing.com

Printed in the United States of America

ISBN 978-1-966075-04-2

Library of Congress Control Number: 2025932129

Fiction: Short Story Collection

Gnashing Teeth Publishing First Edition

# The Lighthouse Keeper

Stories

by

Alex Haber

# Table of Contents

To Danielle, Malcolm, and Evelyn

# Homeless

It was the way her body felt on the sand, she said. It didn't feel nice. If they maybe had a blanket, or something to set down…but the young man had gone off without responding, leaving her alone on a shadowed stretch of beach in late autumn.

Beyond the rocks, the sun stood over the lake, casting its bright orange glare along the surface. A cold wind rose and gave the young woman goosebumps. She reached for her shirt. They'd had a nice time on the water that afternoon, swimming despite the season, searching for crayfish and bits of shell along the shore. She hated for things to be like this…the way these things seemed to matter more than anything else. A pair of lake birds circled overhead. She dressed and walked uphill to where the young man had wandered.

At first, she couldn't spot him anywhere. The grass beyond the beach was tall and scraped her feet. She paused to put on her shoes. She thought of calling the young man's name but decided against it. He would be fine. The trail climbed up from the beach, branching out into a series of thin, leafless trees, a distant cliff. Eventually, she found him. He was bending in front of an oak tree on the horizon. She had to squint to see what was happening. An old man, maybe homeless, sat slouched against the tree. He was the only other person they'd seen at the beach all day, and she could just make out his features in the changing light. He seemed to be unconscious. She watched from a distance as the young man reached toward the old man. When he rose again, he carried a large, green bottle that reflected the sun.

"What are you doing?" she asked, catching up. He drank from the bottle, arching his back in a proud way, and handed it to her.

"He won't miss it," he said.

"Is he..."

"Passed out. Drunk." He drank long and thirsty from the bottle, wiping his lips, and offered it again, but she wouldn't accept it.

"You *drove* us here," she said.

"I'll drive us back."

"No," she said. She walked away from the man against the tree, not toward the car or the beach, but across the hill, the tall, sharp grass. Her hair blew in the wind, and she tried to hold it down. She didn't hear the young man's footsteps behind her. He was probably still drinking. Fine. It was freezing and she didn't want to walk. It was all so difficult. Eventually, she heard him catching up.

"You're not thirsty?" he said.

She didn't answer. They walked single file down the field, not talking, until they reached the cliff overlooking the lake. A cold breeze rippled the vast, orange water.

"I don't know why you have to act this way," she said. "You know I want it the same as you."

The young man kept on drinking. He stood on the edge of the cliff, his back to the young woman.

"But you won't talk. You never talk. You storm off and act crazy. You steal and you drink, and you say you want to drive us home. Can't we just have a nice time for a change and leave it at that?"

"How can you say that?" he said, turning around. "That you want it, too?"

"I *do*," she said.

He laughed.

"Not here. On the ground. Without privacy."

"There's no one around!"

"What about the old man at the tree?" she said. From the top of the cliff, they could still make him out, a short, brownish growth beside the tree trunk.

The young man moved toward the young woman, and she pushed him away.

"Not here and not anywhere," he said. "I've given you all the time in the world. I took you to the beach in October. You're selfish." He approached her again, wetting his lips. She reached into his pocket and took his keys.

"Give them back," he said.

She ran toward the parking lot. She heard him behind her, not close, but taking his time. She got in and locked the door. When the young man arrived, he started banging on the glass.

She turned on the ignition, but she couldn't drive away. Instead, she buried her face in the steering wheel and waited for him to stop. He would stop at some point. He always did. He would calm down and get over it. She would drive them back to town and park his father's car at his parents' house and walk the half-mile down the road in the cold. The next day he would call her at home, and he would come over and maybe he would apologize. It wasn't unthinkable. Or maybe, after all this, she would just give in and let him have it in her room, and she would bite her tongue and just be done with it. It wouldn't kill her. She listened to the bottle smash and shatter on the concrete. The sun went down, and the sky filled with stars. Out here, at the beach, the stars came early. The young man settled, and the girl let him in. She turned on the car's headlights and checked the mirrors. Driving away, she saw the small, shrinking image of the old man behind her. He had risen from his tree and was standing hunched over the field, wildly searching through the tall grass all around him.

# A Story About Rain

Spring came, but the birds did not return to the city. It looked like rain, though it might have been slush (or it might have been nothing). It had been a harsh winter in Chicago, and though it was April, the cold air lingered like the end of a sickness. Kathy sat in the window, reading a book of short stories. She'd read them all before—one of these days she would buy more books, maybe a whole library's worth: she liked to read, didn't she, but she couldn't go out today. Instead, she watched the clock. She tried to spot the sun behind the clouds. She wondered about her cat, Lucy, whom she'd pushed out onto the fire escape the week before. She wished she could go back to sleep.

*

Down on the street, a man with snow-white hair and a tattered overcoat stumbled through the city. He carried a box, clumsily wrapped. He wore thin shoes soaked in the puddles of yesterday's rain. In the hand not holding the box, he wielded a cane, and when he looked up at the buildings, his glasses slid down his face.

It made him sad to come to the city, and the traveling was treacherous. But it was his duty to come here, despite his wife's concerns.

"You're not helping anyone," she said. "Especially when you insist on getting lost along the way."

In fact, he was lost right now, shivering in the cold. He watched a young man walking by. Everyone in the city was so young now. The sounds of the old man's sloshing feet and cane came to a stop.

"Excuse me," he said to the young man on the sidewalk.

He got no reply.

The old man considered letting him go. He could find another stranger…perhaps this man was in a hurry. But he was late himself, and his feet were aching. He tried again.

"Excuse me," he repeated.

This time the young man turned. He took a drag from a small, metallic device and blew a cloud of smoke into the air.

"I'm wondering," said the old man, "if you can point me in the direction of Monroe Boulevard. I'm looking for the Fair Tower Apartments."

"Monroe?" said the young man. "Fair Tower?" He looked down at his phone. He was handsome and blonde, well dressed, the way his son had used to be.

"You turn down the next street," he pointed. "Then you cut left on Washington, two blocks north. It's on the right, about another block."

The old man followed the pointing finger. He squinted in the wind and made a slow nod of understanding.

"Thank you," he replied.

The young man turned and blew another smoke cloud.

"Excuse me," said the old man again, leaning on his cane. "I don't mean to be a bother; you've been so kind already. But I don't suppose you could walk with me the rest of the way, if it's not too far? I came here for a meeting, and I'm afraid I'm late."

The young man looked down as if trying to understand. "I have to get somewhere. But follow those instructions. Left, left, right. You've got it."

This time he didn't let the old man respond but continued down the sidewalk. The old man leaned and watched him go, watching the gray smoke blend into the air.

*

When she heard the knock on the door, Kathy was nearly asleep. At first she'd forgotten what the knocking had meant. She checked the clock and hurried, setting her book down on the sill. She fixed her hair with her fingers along the way.

"Martin," she exclaimed at the old man in the doorway.

As always, she was breathless at his appearance. It was uncanny, the similarities. She could barely stand the sight of him.

"Afternoon, Katherine. I'm sorry I'm late."

They embraced in the doorway, like two old friends, and she took the old man's jacket, cold and damp from the city.

"I was only just reading. Please come in."

She took him to his favorite seat, a recliner in the corner that was otherwise unused.

"I haven't made any reservations," she said. "I thought we could just order in this year."

"That sounds fine, dear," said Martin. "It's *your* birthday. Which reminds me..." he held out the tall, wine-shaped box.

"Oh, Martin," she said in a humorous voice, "you always know just what to get me."

In the kitchen, she washed a pair of glasses. She called into the next room.

"The weather is just awful, isn't it? We could have rescheduled, you know? Has it started to rain yet?"

"Not yet," he said. "Could be any minute, though." He took off his shoes and set them beside the recliner. When Kathy returned, she found him rubbing his wet, socked feet.

"What do you think, Martin? Do you like pepperoni?"

"Whatever you like, dear."

She unwrapped the box as she dialed and talked into the phone. She was barefoot, still in her pajamas, and she sat across the coffee table on the sofa.

"So," said Kathy, setting down the phone. Martin did not look up but continued his ardent rubbing. His face was icy and serious. Kathy took the opportunity to watch him, to study his familiar mannerisms. She had to turn away. "How's Sue?"

"Sue's fine, thank you. She says hello."

"You tell her the same. Is she still playing organ on Sundays?"

"No, not lately, dear. The arthritis." He held up his wrinkled hands and looked up at the ceiling. "I told her, He'll understand."

Kathy smiled. "I'm sorry to hear that."

"She's a fighter, you know. She sends her love."

"I know," said Kathy.

"I hope you like the wine. I got help picking it out."

"It looks wonderful," said Kathy. "Thank you." She poured two glasses and they both had a sip.

"Tell me," said Martin. "How are you, really? How is everything? How is your work?"

"It's fine," she said. "All of it fine."

"That's good. And have you been keeping company?"

She flushed and shook her head. "I'd hardly have the time."

"I see."

"Right now, I'm mostly worried about Lucy."

"Lucy?"

"Our cat. The old cat. You remember."

"Of course. Where is the tabby?"

"She ran off, actually. Not too long ago."

"Ran off? That's a shame. You'd had her as long as I remember."

He frowned across the table. "John wanted a pet growing up. But Sue was allergic."

"I know," said Kathy.

"A shame," he repeated. "How did it happen?"

Kathy shrugged. "Just one of those things."

Outside, the cold wind howled through the street. They listened to the traffic.

"You know," he said, "Sue doesn't usually let me eat pepperoni."

"I don't usually eat it myself," said Kathy.

*

Martin left before sundown. He had to walk to the train and drive from the station back to his home in Michigan City. When he left, his coat was still frigid, his shoes wet.

"Listen," said Martin, "I want you to have a good birthday. And many more."

"Thank you, Martin," said Kathy.

They said their goodbyes in the doorway. She could hardly look him in the eye, but their hug was long and firm. It left her shaking.

"Next year," he said. And with a wink, he disappeared into the hallway and was gone.

Alone in her apartment, Kathy hid behind the door.

*Next year*, she repeated.

She thought to watch him out the window, to see him shrink away into the afternoon, still not raining but looking just as threatening as before. Instead, she stood very still.

When the phone rang, Kathy jumped. She went to the kitchen, stopping at the table for another sip of wine.

"Hello?" she said.

"Is he gone," came the voice.

"Yes. Just now."

"Are you okay?"

"Yes, it was fine."

"At least it's over."

"I know."

She was close to tears now.

"Alright," said the man. "I'll pick you up for dinner."

"Okay."

"It's your birthday, you know? Let's have some fun."

"I know. I want to."

"Okay. I love you. I'll see you soon."

"Okay. I love you, too."

# Shade

The sun couldn't reach us in the woods, so we didn't spend much time there. We liked it in the sun. We liked the river. We liked to sweat and to peel the thin, dead skin from our bodies and sprinkle it around. Like snakes, we shed along the muddy river. Like plants, we came alive in the sun.

Mikey took the first shot. He missed by a mile.

"The sun's too bright."

"If you say so," I said.

We were standing in the tall grass by the river. We faced the woods.

"Do-over," he said.

This time he missed by half-a-mile.

"Nice one," I said.

"You try, if you're so damn amazing."

"He ain't bothering me," I said.

Mikey spit on the grass. A thick, gooey ball. I watched it pop and spread on the dirt.

"How are you so good at that?"

"Easy," said Mikey.

"I never have enough spit."

"You've got to bring it up–like this."

He made a phlegmy sound, loud and guttural. It must have come from deep inside. He was always making that sound.

I tried, too. "Still nothing."

"You're scared," said Mikey.

"Of spitting?"

"Of throwing. No way you can get closer than me."

"So why try?"

He made the sound again–it echoed down the field, along the river. He searched for rocks.

I looked at the spit, still foaming. I was standing at the threshold of the woods, the line on the grass where the sun turned to shade. It was colder in the woods than by the river. We walked home for dinner through the woods at night. It was the only time of day we didn't talk much.

"You're a sad excuse for a hobo," said Mikey. "It's a good thing your parents got dough. You'd never make it in the wild for real. I'd give you a week."

"I'd give you a day."

"I'm not the one who's scared," he said.

"Me either."

"So, take a shot." He handed me a rock.

"Not *that* one. It's too good for skipping."

"Then here."

 "That one's way bigger than yours was."

"So find your own, Goldilocks."

I pretended to comb through the grass. The spit was still bubbling, leaving a darkish stain on the dirt.

"Here," said Mikey. He shoved a small rock in my hand.

"Fine," I said. I took position. In doing so, I covered up the spit with dirt. I don't know why. I brought my arm back and fired.

"Damn," I said.

"You missed by a *football field.*"

"Whatever."

"It didn't even flinch."

"It didn't flinch at yours either."

"Yeah it did."

"Let's go swimming," I said.

"I'm starving. I got to eat something."

"Then let's go fishing."

"I told you, my stomach can't take no more fish."

"We're out of rocks anyway."

"Here," said Mikey. "You go first. We'll each take one more try."

"Come on. There's hardly any meat on him."

"Just throw."

I lifted the rock and aimed more carefully. This time, it bounced off a tree and skittered through the shade.

"You're missing on purpose," said Mikey. "No way you suck *that* bad."

"I'm sweaty. It's hot as hell."

Mikey took his turn. I almost didn't watch. It was a good shot, seeming to fly forever, moving through the air like a magnet.

"Shit," I said.

Mikey hollered. He gurgled and spit again and ran through the woods.

"Did you kill him?" I said.

"I don't know," he called. "I can't find it."

"Maybe you missed."

"Hell no. I hit it dead-on. You saw."

"I couldn't tell."

"It's got to be here somewhere."

"He probably ran off."

"Oh shit."

Mikey bent over. I ran in to see. The chipmunk was breathing. There was blood on his head and in the grass. His eye was big and low. A cloud of gnats was already hovering.

"I told you I got him."

"He's not dead," I said.

"Not yet. But I got him in the temple. See? Good thing, too. Now we won't go hungry."

"We just ate lunch, you idiot."

"You're crazy. It's been days."

"He's twitching."

"I call *this* part."

"We should do something."

"Like what?"

"I don't know. Step on him?"

"Me?" said Mikey.

"You're the one who shot him."

"You're the one with shoes on."

I looked at my feet. "So, go get yours."

"I don't know where I left them. It'll have to be you."

The chipmunk faced the river. It was a hot, sunny day. The sun shined in thick, yellow rays on the river. Normally, you couldn't see the sun rays, but today you could see them from the woods. The shaking got worse.

"You do it," I said. I took off my shoes.

"They're too small for me."

The chipmunk made a clicking noise.

"Just do it," I said.

I turned and left toward the river. I sat in the grass. I ripped blades of grass from the dirt. I jumped in the river. The water was hot. I went underneath. You couldn't see below the surface because of all the mud. I counted to thirty and came back up. I went down again. This time, I counted to ten. I got out and sat on the grass again and looked at the sun. The sun is 94 million miles from the earth, but it was still hot and bright out that day. It felt good to sit there in the sun.

Mikey came back and dropped my shoes.

"Where is it?" I said.

"Back there."

"Did you do it?"

"I told you, they're too small."

"Is he still shaking?"

"I don't know."

We sat there with our feet in the water. It was about one o'clock in the afternoon, the sun just a little to the side.

"You think there's a heaven for chipmunks?" said Mikey.

"I hope so," I said.

"I doubt it."

"I bet there is."

"And a hell?"

"I guess so. Probably."

"What would a chipmunk *do* to go to hell?"

We laughed.

"If there's no chipmunk hell," he said, "there's no chipmunk heaven."

"Why not?"

"Because there can't be a heaven without a hell. It's all or nothing."

We sat there by the river.

We looked at the river.

We sat in the sun.

# Safari

A couple walks into an oyster bar in Michigan. It is nighttime, snowing, they stamp their feet. The man orders oysters at the bar, holds up two fingers for beer. The bar is cold and dimly lit, and the couple leans on the counter. A baseball game plays overhead.

*David:* Can you see who's winning?

*Alison:* I don't know. Not us.

Their beers come and the couple starts drinking.

*David:* You look like you're gonna be sick.

*Alison:* I'm just not hungry. You know, like I said.

*David:* Come on, they're not so bad. Look, there's hot sauce and lemons, if you want.

*Alison:* That seems somehow worse.

*David:* You'll like them, I promise.

*Alison.* I'll pass.

*David:* How can you know if you don't try?

*Alison:* I know what I like.

*David:* You can't know for sure if you've never tried them. There was once a time in your life when you'd never tried pizza, right? Or beer?

*Alison:* Doesn't ring a bell. Anyway, you can have them all.

*David:* I don't need that many oysters. I ordered enough for both of us.

*Alison:* We'll take some home.

*David:* Now you're being silly.

*Alison:* That's me—silly.

*David:* One of the many reasons I love you.

*Alison:* How sweet.

*David:* I wish you were in a better mood, though. We're doing something different for a change. It's fun.

*Alison:* I'm in a good mood. I'm drinking.

*David:* Try just one for me. It's easy, I promise. Just close your eyes and down the hatch. Like a shot.

*Alison:* If I have to.

*David:* Yes, you have to.

*Alison:* Alright, just for you.

*David:* If you want to spit it up, you can.

*Alison:* I will.

*David:* Okay.

They drink beer in silence. Alison watches the bartender, a middle-aged woman in a button-up shirt. She has no other customers but seems a world away. As Alison watches, David looks at the TV, craning his neck.

*David:* Did something happen?

*Alison:* Who knows. I think it's a strike-out.

*David:* On who?

*Alison:* I don't know. Do you want to trade seats?

*David:* No, it doesn't matter.

*Alison:* Did you know they eat scorpions in China?

*David:* Yeah, we watched that movie together.

*Alison:* And calves' brains in France. And remember my Uncle Mark? When he used to go hunting up north, he'd use every part of the deer, like the Indians. He even ate the dick.

*David:* What? Why?

*Alison:* Because otherwise it's wasteful. Anyway, some people like it.

*David:* If you say so.

*Alison:* What about you? Would you eat a scorpion for me?

*David:* It's not the same thing.

*Alison:* What if I asked you nicely? Would you eat a dick for me, love?

*David:* You don't have to try one. It's not a big deal.

*Alison:* I know, but I'd hate to disappoint you.

*David:* I'll eat them fast and we can go.

*Alison:* I don't want to go. It's nice in here.

*David:* It's freezing.

*Alison:* Would you like my coat?

*David:* You're funny.

*Alison:* No, silly.

*David:* You're ridiculous.

*Alison:* I'm serious. I like it here. And look, we have the whole place to ourselves.

*David:* If you say so.

*Alison:* I do.

*David:* Let's at least get more of these.

*Alison:* Fine by me.

They look for the bartender, but the room is now empty.

*David:* Where'd she go?

*Alison:* The kitchen. I can kind of see her.

*David:* Can you get her attention?

*Alison:* I think you'd have better luck.

*David:* I don't think so.

*Alison:* You have a way with waitresses.

*David:* Here she comes.

David orders two more beers.

*Alison:* For someone her age, she's pretty, don't you think?

*David:* I didn't notice.

*Alison:* Her hair is so blonde. I wish I was blonde.

*David:* They need to take out Terry. He's throwing for shit.

*Alison:* I think I'd look good blonde, don't you?

*David:* I like your hair.

*Alison:* It's okay to like blondes. I think I'll try it sometime. For you.

*David:* Maybe you don't need another round.

*Alison:* Too late.

*Bartender:* Your oysters will be up in a minute.

*David:* Thank you.

*Alison:* She's a perfect waitress, don't you think?

*David:* Did you hear that Andy's going on safari next week?

*Alison:* He is?

*David:* I'm jealous.

*Alison:* A safari sounds amazing. I wish we could go.

*David:* Maybe we can go somewhere fun over the holidays.

*Alison:* That's so far away. I wish we could go somewhere tonight. To Egypt.

*David:* We'd have to get shots for Africa. Andy came in all bandaged up.

*Alison:* It doesn't have to be Africa. How about something simple? The Grand Canyon. Neither of us have ever been. Or Yosemite. Mount Rushmore.

*David:* I've been to Yosemite and Mount Rushmore. When I was little.

*Alison:* I didn't know that. Which one was better?

*David:* I don't know. I didn't really care when I was seven.

*Alison:* Little seven-year-old David.

*David:* I was an awful kid.

*Alison:* All kids are awful.

*David:* Some more than others.

*Alison:* All children are awful. I would never have one.

*David:* Fine by me.

*Alison:* I'm glad that's settled.

*David:* Same.

*Alison:* I just want to get away from Michigan.

*David:* I want to eat.

*Alison:* Good thing you ordered so many oysters.

*David:* Do you want to go anywhere after this?

*Alison:* Wherever you'd like. It's still early.

*David:* Nowhere in particular.

*Alison:* We could ask our waitress what time she gets off.

*David:* Okay.

*Alison:* She's more your type than mine, though.

*David:* You're the one who keeps bringing her up.

*Alison:* I couldn't be that forward with someone I just met. I guess we're different that way.

*David:* I wish we were going to Africa with Andy.

*Alison:* Is Jenna going?

*David:* No. He's going with some guys from work. I don't think she's into the idea.

*Alison:* I'm sure she'll find something to do while he's away.

*David:* You're relentless, you know that?

*Alison:* I just meant maybe a girls' night. Now who's being paranoid?

*David:* It was just the one time, Allie. We talked about this. How many times can I say I'm sorry? What do I have to do to make you believe it?

*Alison:* Don't get upset.

*David:* If I wasn't so hungry, I'd say we should leave.

*Alison:* Poor, hungry man.

*David:* We'll go after the oysters.

*Alison:* All twelve of them.

*David:* I could probably eat a hundred.

*Alison:* Good, here she comes.

The waitress sets down a large plate of oysters. The dish is sprinkled with rows of ice, shining lemon wedges, an unlabeled sauce.

*Alison:* Just look at them.

*David:* Let me know if you change your mind.

*Alison:* No way.

*David:* Are you sure?

*Alison:* I wouldn't want to deprive my hungry man.

*David:* Appreciate it. Can you see the score?

*Alison:* Nothing's changed.

*David:* Christ. Well, bottoms up.

# Light Glinting on the Shattered Glass of a Thousand Caved-In Malls in Missouri

It wasn't such a big deal, what they did to her. It was a joke. Anyway, she was a punk girl. She had tattoos. Of course, they learned the truth about those–the fountain washed her arms clean. She coughed a bunch during the baptism, probably from the chemicals or rust. The fountain had been out of commission for months now.

Her nipple rings were real, though.

"You cold or something?" said someone. They pointed their flashlights and laughed.

"You mean these?"

She lifted her shirt. (You see? She was a punk girl.)

"Did it hurt?"

"Like hell," she said. "You know how many nerves are in your tits?"

Her clothes were wet, and she was barefoot, like the rest of them, their sneakers all strewn in the darkness.

She put down her shirt.

"So, am I in the group or what?"

It was noon, though it could've been midnight, it was so dark in the mall. If you went down that way and turned right, where the Little Caesars used to be, you could see the sun coming in through the plywood. But down here, on the west end, it was black. You couldn't see anything. A galaxy of flashlights lit the scene.

"Not yet," said someone.

They turned on a radio, but the signal was bad.

"Shut it off," said someone.

"We need music for the next part."

"Next part?" she said. "Can't we hurry this along?"

"You got somewhere to be?"

"Maybe I do."

"Let's hear your pipes."

"You know I can sing."

"I told you," said someone, "she complains about everything."

"Fine. Which song?"

"How about the Kennedys? 'Too Drunk to Fuck.'"

"Acapella?"

"If you don't want to, we can find someone else."

"Whatever." She sang the song.

"Louder!" they shouted.

She screamed the lyrics, putting on a show, using her flashlight as a microphone. When she finished, they clapped.

"I'm hard as hell," said someone.

They laughed.

"Prove it," she said.

The room went quiet. They turned to the boy.

"You haven't earned the right," he said.

"Don't be a chicken. I showed you mine."

"Not the *good* stuff."

"Okay, chicken."

"You go all the way first, then."

"Yeah right."

"You *said* you wanted to see mine. So come on."

"Hell no. I don't actually want to see it."

"Why not?"

"Because they're gross."

"I told you she was one of them."

"No, I just think they're ugly."

"That's because you haven't seen mine."

"Come on. Aren't you guys supposed to be different?"

"Different how?"

"I don't know. You go to Catholic school."

"So what?"

"I don't know. I just thought you'd be…Catholic."

"No way. Fuck that shit."

"Then why did I have to get baptized?"

"We just wanted to get your shirt wet."

They laughed. The echoes filled the room. It seemed to come from everywhere. This was dumb. Of course, it was like this. She should have known better.

"Happy hour," said someone.

"I have to go," she said.

"What's your hurry?"

"I didn't think this would take all day. It's just some shitty punk band."

"Who are you calling shitty?"

"We *are* shitty, dude."

"Fuck you. We're the fastest punk band in Eastmont."

"You're the *only* punk band in Eastmont," she said. "And who ever heard of a band without a singer? You *need* me. So shut the fuck up and no more rituals. I'm in the band."

"Alright. But you have to have a beer with us. To make it official."

They passed around a plastic bag.

"Fucking Catholics and your ceremonies," she said.

"In the name of the Father, the Son…"

She grabbed a bottle with the intent to chug it, but the cap wouldn't twist. Someone shot a flashlight in her eyes.

"Like this," he said.

He ran and smashed the bottle on the edge of the fountain. It exploded and shot foam everywhere.

"You're an idiot," said someone.

"Who brings beers that aren't twist-offs?"

"It's all they had in the garage, asshole."

"I know another trick," she said. "Who's got a lighter?" They turned their attention. "Watch this." She held a lighter upside down, using its corner to pry the ridges of the cap. Eventually, it sprung off like a cork, ricocheting somewhere in the shadows. Everyone cheered.

"That settles it," said someone. "I'm in love."

They took turns popping open bottles and singing songs. As they did, she snuck off down the hall. It was almost too dark to see. She poured some of her beer out on the floor.

She remembered this place. She came here all the time when she was little. Her mom would get haircuts at the salon. There was a candy machine in the salon, and she would beg her mom for a quarter, then sit by the magazines and chomp. Her mom's hair was lovely. It always smelled like fruits. She could picture it on the floor of the salon, in long, silky curls. She would give anything for a jar of those clippings.

She finished the rest of the beer on her own. It was nasty and warm. But she'd earned it. When someone grabbed her from behind, she jumped.

"You're all wet," said the voice.

"No shit. It's from the fountain."

His hand moved down her back. She elbowed him, hard. He let out a noise.

"What's going on over there?" said someone. "You guys want privacy?"

"I'm going," she said. "I'll see you at practice."

"Hang on, you can't leave."

"Watch me."

"There's one more thing you have to do."

"Just text me later."

Someone else grabbed her from behind.

"It won't take long," said someone.

"I'm quick."

She felt their hands on her body but managed to wriggle free. She cracked the nearest boy with her bottle. It blew up on his forehead. Whoever it was screamed like bloody murder.

"What did you do that for?"

While they shouted, she slipped down the hallway, finding her way without a flashlight.

Outside, the daylight was blinding. She realized her shoes were still back there but tossed the broken bottle on the ground and pedaled home.

*

The house was empty, as usual. There was a note from her dad on the counter. Some money for pizza. She left it and went to her room. She turned on a Bikini Kill CD and cranked it so loud the house shook. It was the one good thing about living alone…or practically. She screamed along, punching the hell out of her pillows and sheets. When it ended, she felt better. Sort of dizzy. She noticed a stain on the carpet. It was on her bed, too. She looked down and saw a piece of glass sticking out of her heel. It was a big one, shiny and green. How had she not felt it? It looked pretty deep. The blood was still trickling.

With a deep breath, she yanked it out, plugging the cut with a sock.

# Under the Pier

We left school early to go down to the pier. It was there in the morning the fishmongers parked their boats and unloaded. Danny said it smelled like sex, but in the afternoon the docks were dry and specked with old folks, the wafting flags of severed fishing lines stuck to wooden posts.

It was Hannah's idea to ditch. "I want to show you something," she'd said. "You trust me, right?"

I thought of Danny. He wasn't an expert on most things, but he was dating Katie Miller at the time, and you couldn't call bullshit on things you knew nothing about.

We snuck out after fourth period. Along the way, she even held my hand.

"You're sweaty," she said.

When we got there, I figured we'd go up the pier, but instead, she took me underneath. To be honest, I would have followed her anywhere. She took off her shoes by the tide. Beneath the pier, it was dark and foamy. She led me in. We sloshed through the waves with heavy steps.

"Thanks for coming," she said. "What do you think?"

The docks creaked above us, probably the weight of old fishermen. The smell was rotten, almost tangy. A single line of sunlight leaked through the floorboards,  drawing a path from Hannah's temple to her lips.

"I like it," I said.

"Most people are too chicken to come," she said. "Are you ready?"

"Chicken?" I said. Her lips were quivering. She closed her eyes. She counted to three.

Then, she started screaming.

"What's wrong?" I said.

She wouldn't stop. The sound was piercing and shook everything around us. I covered my ears. I imagined the old folks on the pier, startled and peering through the slats.

"Hannah?" I shouted.

She was smiling. Suddenly, another screeching took over. It was a second voice, as high as Hannah's. They sounded in conversation. She stopped and ducked and pulled me toward her. I nearly fell in the lake. By accident, I touched her chest. I felt hard cotton.

"What's going on?" I asked. Something brushed my neck. Then another. I held her more tightly, and over the screeching, I could hear her wild laugh.

A series of bats flew out from the pier, at first in single file, then all at once. They burst toward the ocean, hitting the sunlight, and curving west.

The whole time, Hannah was cheering. In the commotion, I again touched her padding. She was overwhelmed and ignored me completely.

When the last bat disappeared, she stood upright.

"Have you ever seen anything like it?" she gasped.

I shook my head.

"Look! You have goosebumps!"

"I do?"

My ears were ringing. I leaned in to kiss her, unable to resist, but at the same time, she turned away and headed for the beach. I watched her go, unmoving. The air was sick with smell.

# Tick

That summer the sun was a crankshaft, turning loudly, getting hotter all the time.

We ate sandwiches by the river. Never mind that hobos don't eat sandwiches. We took turns staring at the sun, trying to see who could last the longest.

"What the hell?" said Mikey.

There was something on my leg. It was moving back and forth. At first I thought it was a sun hallucination.

"Whoa, that's a big one," said Mikey.

"What the hell is it?"

"It's a tick."

"It looks like it's trying to get inside me."

"It is. You better get it out. If you don't you'll get diseased."

I started clawing.

"Not like that," he laughed. He was on his hands and knees, inspecting the tick up close.

"If you hit it too hard, you'll break its head off. It'll get stuck inside your leg and keep eating."

"What do I do?"

"You've got to pinch your skin. Like this."

He did it on his belly, bare and lean.

"Use your nails to work the blood out. You have to drown the sucker, really blast it."

Its tiny legs were cycling. Blood was dripping down my leg. I tried to wipe it off, but when I did, I brushed too hard and the body ripped clean off, just like Mikey had said. Its head was still in there. A tiny speck.

"Shit."

"You blew it."

"What do I do now?"

"Nothing you *can* do. But don't worry. It'll die before long."

He lay on the grass, stretched out and sunny. The sun was still grinding. It sounded like a room of machines, pumping, jacking.

I got up and washed in the river. I could see the minuscule head still there in my skin, like a bud of hair. I squeezed and pinched at my leg until it was raw. The thing wouldn't budge.

"I told you not to flick it," said Mikey.

"How the hell do you know so much about it?"

"I've had plenty of ticks."

I'd never seen Mikey with a tick before. He was full of crazy stories, never mind that he'd lived here all his life.

"Did you get diseased?"

"Hell no. I got them out."

"Am I gonna get sick?"

He shrugged. "My brother got one stuck once. He was fine after a while. But it's still there to this day. It's on the bottom of his foot."

We lay there by the river in the sun. There weren't any clouds out, just the sun, hot and grinding. I rubbed my leg again. It started to hurt.

"You should name it," said Mikey.

I laughed. "I'll call him Mikey."

"What about Lou? That sounds like a hobo's name."

"Okay."

It stayed in my leg all summer, below the skin. It was the three of us, me and Mikey and Lou. The sun kept churning, producing more heat.

Sometimes I wonder if it's still in there, under the hair. Maybe over time it absorbed into my body and now I'm part-man, part-tick.

More likely it got eaten by bacteria. Flushed out. I don't know. I'm not a scientist.

# Kids

Billy Turner worked at the mall before it shut down. He had a job in sales, or so he said. In truth, he sold weed in the stairwell behind JC Penney. His storefront was the kiddie park with all the plastic rides, kids climbing up the snail's back, sliding down the dog's truck. He sat on a nearby bench and waited for clients. He watched the kids playing while he sat. He liked to watch. They had fun doing nothing. Their brains were so minuscule at that age. It was funny. There were all kinds of kids at the kiddie park, Black and white and Latino and Asian. Some had moms who stuck around and watched. Some had moms who dropped them off and left to get their nails done or whatever. It pissed Billy off, the moms who dumped their kids and vanished, like the world wasn't some terrible, dangerous place. One of these days he would teach them a lesson. It would be so easy. Sometimes a kid came right up to him, to show off his missing tooth or weird dinosaur shirt. He didn't know why they picked him. Maybe he had a trusting face. He looked like a kid himself—which, technically, he was. Maybe their parents just never taught them about strangers. That was a mistake. "I'm a friend of your cousin," he might say. "I live on your street and your mom asked me to take you home." That would teach them. You shouldn't leave a kid at the mall all by himself. Kids are dumb as hell. They'll believe fucking anything. How did these people even become parents? You should have to pass a test. It wasn't a hard job to watch a kid. He did it all the time, waiting for his clients.

He had lots of clients. He called them his "clients" and not his "customers" because "customers" implies a one-time relationship. "Clients" are people who keep coming back. That's what Billy said. He did good business at the mall. There was almost no security there. It wasn't a very nice mall. It sure looked fun to be a kid. He couldn't remember being one himself. Had he ever played on the mall rides? He doubted it. His grandma could barely get around. He didn't have memories of the snail slide or dog truck. It was funny to watch the little assholes having fun and making friends with anyone who came by. It was nice. Kids just being kids. They got along with everyone. It didn't matter what you looked like or where you came from. At least at that age. They only wanted to play. He could watch them for hours, between sales, and sometimes he did. They laughed like little dumbasses and cried whenever they fell, which was funny as hell to watch. He had to be careful not to laugh too loud, or the moms who actually stuck around would notice. They might ask questions about what the hell he was doing there, a teenager hanging around at a kiddie park, with baggy jeans and lip rings, with nothing to do. On top of that, his leg was always shaking. That he couldn't help. It was chronic. A medical condition. Or it would've been if he'd actually been diagnosed. His grandma didn't have any insurance. It wasn't a big deal. He was used to it. It didn't hurt, it just made him look kind of nervous. He wasn't nervous though. Why should he be? Selling weed was easy. It practically sold itself. All he had to do was sit and wait.

Now and then he went to the stairwell. He didn't smoke weed himself. Sometimes he thought about it. It might help with his leg or pass the time. His friends all smoked, but Billy was just in it for the cash. He wasn't so good at school. He couldn't rely on his smarts for opportunities, not with his lousy attention span or those crummy teachers who didn't give a shit who passed or failed, who lived or died. He wasn't so good at making stuff with his hands or talking to people either. That's why selling weed was perfect. No sales pitch required. Just make your presence known. At least to the right people. Then it's all about waiting, going to the stairwell, and swapping a little baggie for cash. One green thing for another. It was simple. His clients liked that he didn't fuck around. Sometimes they wanted to smoke with him. Stoners were friendly that way. He liked that. His mom had ruined weed for him. She'd ruined lots of stuff. Also, he'd made a promise to his grandma that he wouldn't mess around with that stuff. Not after his mom. His grandma was smart as hell. She'd smell it on him. She'd whip his ass or worse, she'd start crying. He couldn't take that again.

His grandma was tough. She'd raised her kids while working full-time. Now she was raising him too—as much she could or needed to. He was practically raised at this point. But he didn't want to see her cry. It was a shitty thing to see. Even though weed, he knew, wasn't all that bad. His friends told him it was no worse than beer. "And you drink beer, don't you?" Sure he did, but that was beer. His mom didn't drink beer. She didn't crash into a median after drinking Bud Lite. She could've though—weed's less impairing than alcohol, they said. That wasn't the point. He'd made a promise. "So why sell it?" The truth is, he didn't like selling it either, but what choice did he have? Anyway, it wasn't his problem what people chose to buy. That was capitalism. America. He watched the kids on the mall rides. One of these days he'd do it. It would be easy. Almost no one was watching. He sized one up, a chubby kid sitting on the dragon ride. No one was watching him except Billy. He was wearing Nikes. Billy had never owned Nikes before. What kind of mom bought her kid Nikes and then left him all alone at the mall? It was crazy.

As if sensing his interest, the little kid came over. He could've been four or six or ten—Billy had no idea about kids. He didn't know any in person, and he couldn't remember being one himself. Maybe he never was one.

The kid looked up at the bench, biting his lip.

"What's that?" he said.

Billy looked down. A dime bag was hanging from his pocket. He covered it up. He looked around but of course no one was paying attention.

"It's nothing," said Billy.

The kid turned around.

"Actually," said Billy, "it's candy."

"What kind?"

"What kind do you like?"

"Chocolate. And caramel."

"You're in luck. This is a chocolate-caramel candy. I'll let you have it, if you want."

"It doesn't look like chocolate."

"It's a new kind."

"What kind?"

"It's the best kind in the world. It's like M&Ms and Reese's and Snickers all combined. I can let you have it if you want it. But you have to follow the rules."

"Okay."

"You can't open it here. You have to give it to your mom to open when she gets back."

"Why?"

"Because it's hard to open. It's childproof, you know? The company has to do it that way. Otherwise, kids would eat it all the time and get sick. That's how good it is. You get it?"

He nodded.

"Make sure you hide it. The other kids will try to steal it. They'll kick your ass and take it. So put it in your pocket and give it to your mom when she comes back. Tell her an old guy gave it to you, okay? A really old guy."

The little kid stuck it in his pocket and went back to the playground.

Billy got the hell out of there. He went outside and laughed his ass off. It was priceless—easy as hell. He didn't even care about the money. He could make more later. There were always more clients. He pictured the shitty mom's face.

*

When the mall closed for good, Billy moved to the park on Clinton Street—a real outdoor park with swings and trees. He could've gone to lots of places, but it's what he was used to. It was a good cover, anyway, hiding out in the open. Plus, he liked kids. They were always having fun. He tried like hell to remember what it was like to be one. He must've at least come to a park before.

It was the same thing at the park though—parents would drop their kids off and go play tennis, run laps around the baseball diamond. That summer he tried an experiment. He took a little girl. He planned it out in advance and everything. He chose the right one. She was always there, and her mom was never around. He had some beers first, to get his head straight.

"I'm here to pick you up," he said. "Your mom's at the toy store. She wanted me to get you."

That was it. It was simple. She even held his hand.

He took her to the K-Mart across town and left her there. He went back to the park. He kept his distance from where the parents, and eventually the cops, were standing. They all looked scared as hell.

He thought about trying it again someday. But he needed to give it time. It was easy, but you had to be smart about it. Unfortunately, that summer he got busted for selling weed. The worst part was, he was eighteen now. On the bright side, it meant they didn't have to call his grandma. He called her himself, when he could, from the station, and said he was taking a trip. He did some time in jail. Not too much. It went by fast. While he was there, he thought about the little girl, the chubby kid at the mall. He wondered what the hell had happened to them. It was funny. Those parents would definitely think twice now before leaving them unattended. He'd done good. After all, there were some real fucking creeps out there. During lockup, he made a decision. Selling weed was lousy. From now, on he would only do good.

On his first day out, he went back to the park. He grabbed a little boy this time. It didn't go so well. The damn kid hollered. Billy wasn't sure why. Maybe he didn't look so trusting anymore. The kid kicked and screamed until his parents came over. A bunch of them did. One of them kicked the shit out of Billy. He held him down until the cops showed up. It hurt like hell. Billy wasn't upset though. It only proved his point. It was all because of him. It was his fault the parents had become more attentive, that he was getting his ass kicked. That was good. Next time he would choose a different park though. He would be more careful. It was easy, but you had to be smart about it. It was a good thing he was doing. He would teach them all a lesson. You had to take care of your kids. He was grinning when they put him in the car.

# The Escapist

Dylan Hadley left his wife this morning. In all, he left two children, a ranch-style house in East Bloomfield, a miniature schnauzer with cataracts, and a job teaching math at the local community college.

Mostly, though, he left his wife, Liz Hadley, his companion of fourteen years.

It happened after a brief planning period, not on a whim, as he'd decided to leave a note for Liz to discover. He didn't want her wondering what had happened, hoping for his return. The letter was short and factual, explaining the situation as clearly as he could, and with the right amount of feeling. He'd composed it on the couch the night before, in the glow of the TV, while his wife lay in bed.

The next morning, his plan went into action. He ate a normal breakfast at the table—a bowl of Honey Nut Cheerios, skim milk. He called his kids to get ready for school and made their brown bag lunches. He slipped the note in his wife's purse before heading out the door.

It wasn't the most elegant way to do this, he knew. She would resent him; it was unavoidable. It made him sad, because he loved his wife, and he didn't want to hurt her. In fact, this morning, he loved her more than he had in years. He imagined the look on her face when she discovered the note—at work, maybe, reaching for a pen or snack, sitting in her office, her shoes off, the door open to the world—and the hysterics that would follow, the panic and tears. He felt terrible that it had to happen this way, without more privacy. But he couldn't think of anywhere else to leave the note. It had to be a place where only she would find it, and where it wouldn't be found until after he disappeared. His wife, he knew, was lonely, and tended to follow him around the house. If he felt hungry, she felt hungry too, or in any case, she went to the kitchen.

Every morning, they showered together in their stall of a master bathroom—a habit from the early days, impossible to break. Dylan had spent many showers thinking of his escape. The gradual mundaneness of it all, the lack of intimacy in each other's nude bodies, standing only inches apart or else physically joined because of the limited space, they took turns washing in front of the spray, always Liz before Dylan, then Liz and Dylan again, never making eye contact, never wandering their eyes, or diverting any touch. The process was stoical and unchanging, pragmatically frustrating because of the morning rush, leaving them annoyed with each other, as if the other were nothing but a low-flow shower head, a clogged drain, just another obstacle to deal with before heading off to work.

And so, that morning, he hid the letter in Liz's purse. The bag was slouched on their bed. He tucked it deep inside, where she wouldn't see it until later. He performed the act swiftly, while Liz was in the adjoining bathroom. The night before, he'd barely slept. He thought of her alone in the house, in his absence, like a girl in a maze.

Now the note was hidden. He was about to retreat, to disappear forever, when at the bottom of Liz's purse—a place he'd never gone— beneath the drugstore makeup and phone charger, among the mints and loose change, he felt a shape he didn't recognize. He touched the container, its smooth flat surface. Carefully, he removed it from Liz's purse.

Because he'd memorized his wife's routines, he knew his time was running out. But the pack of cigarettes looked strange in his hands. He knew the brand, the slogan on the box, but it was also alien. He opened the pack; about a third of its contents were missing. He felt around at the bottom of her purse but found none. He lifted the pack to his nose and sniffed the fresh tobacco scent.

The toilet flushed and Dylan hurried. He shoved the box back In the purse, on top of the note he'd written, and mixed up the contents, trying to mask the sound of rustling with the sink. By the time Liz emerged, he'd recovered, and together again, they walked down to the kitchen.

Having made the delivery, Dylan felt eager to escape, but he knew it was important to remain calm. He went about his morning, the adrenaline pumping. He thought of feigning an early meeting, but he didn't want to leave that way, in a hurry. He watched his wife eating. She was beautiful, even now, in her way. The coffee was hot. He kissed his children goodbye, neither of them sparing a glance, and told them to have a good day. He kissed his wife on the corner of her mouth, puckered to receive his lips, and without looking back, he shut the front door behind him.

He had made his escape.

Patiently, he backed out of the driveway. He turned left onto Clarkson, just like any other day.

The subdivision retreated. It had been his home for almost a decade. His body felt weightless, numb.

He thought of the cigarette box.

Why did she have it?

His heart raced. It was only a normal, physical response. The body reacts to stressful situations, even if the situation is right, for the best.

Still, he wondered.

Dylan had smoked a long time ago, back in college, and Liz had nagged him about it until he quit. She hated smokers. There was cancer in her family.

The dashboard clock said *7:18*. She would have left the house by now.

If the cigarettes were hers, she may have already reached into her purse, and if that was the case, she may have already seen the note stashed at the bottom.

But that was fine. Maybe it was better. In her car, having reached for a morning smoke, she would at least be alone. Probably, it shouldn't bother him at all.

She had acted so normal that morning, even kissing him on the lips. He imagined the steps she must have been taking to hide the smell. He'd never so much as caught a whiff of it.

Or had he? He tried to remember. It was impossible to say.

Could they just be someone else's? Was she holding them for someone? Was it some kind of mistake?

He rolled down the window and closed his eyes. Eventually, a loud noise distracted him. A line of cars had formed behind him. Some were blaring their horns, driving past. He watched them go. The light was green. He needed to go, to get out of there. He could find somewhere else to think it over, an empty parking lot or something. Or else he could just go. He had never been freer. But it all seemed so ridiculous.

If she was capable of keeping that secret, what else had she been lying about? And for how long?

He tried to breathe, but the air was hot, and when he looked down at the pedals, they both seemed wrong. The cars continued to honk behind him. He had to go. To just choose a pedal.

The car jerked forward as the light turned red.

# The Lighthouse Keeper

My father had a job as a lighthouse keeper. His lighthouse could be seen from all over town, on account of our town being built on a hill that descended into a lake. But no one was allowed on its grounds but my father. Some said it was haunted. The lighthouse stood close to a hundred feet tall, and according to my father, from the top, you could see the whole town, the way the birds do.

"Nothing goes on in this town without my seeing," said my father.

After dinner, on the night before my thirteenth birthday, we walked down to the lake to skip stones along the surface.

"How can you see anything?" I asked. Not only was my father near-sighted, but the lighthouse was a half-mile from the shore.

My father threw a stone into the lake. *Kerplunk!* From the sand, he opened a beer. He was always doing this, producing beers out of nowhere. He drank it down the way he always did, in long, exaggerated gulps. He took his time. At the end of each drink, he kissed the bottle with a loud pop of his lips. It sounded refreshing.

"You know," he said, looking out at the water, "you can see it for yourself, if you want to."

Digging in the sand, I uncovered a treasure: a smooth thin stone, perfect for skipping. I cleaned it off. I skipped it with a sharp flick of the wrist, the way my father had taught me. It made a few good jumps along the surface of the water.

"Not bad," said my father. At the end of the last skip, after it sank into the lake, a splash came up that formed a series of rings along the surface.

"Fish aren't too smart," I said.

My father shook his head, as if to say he'd known plenty of smart fish. Then he continued. "I'm serious. Would you like to go out to the lighthouse, tonight?"

I glanced in my father's direction. In the setting sun, I could hardly make out the details of his face.

"You're thirteen today," he told me.

"Not till morning."

"Bullshit," he said.

He left the empty bottle and started walking down the shore. Where my father went I followed.

*

The stars came out as we headed toward the boat, which my father kept in a shed down shore. It wasn't our boat; it belonged to the town. I often heard it rumbling, saw it disappear toward the lighthouse, but I'd never been aboard.

The water was freezing. With my pants rolled up, I walked through the tide and tried to adjust to the temperature. My father swatted the air. The mosquitoes had risen and were keeping close by. For some reason, they seemed to like him best.

"You have to keep this a secret," he told me.

"A secret from who?"

He didn't say.

"Even Mom?"

We approached the shed, a ramshackle building.

"This is just between you and me."

My father let ring a loud mosquito-slap as we untied the boat. He jumped into the mud at the bottom of the shack, and there I went behind him.

"We push on three. One, two…"

From a hidden compartment on deck, my father produced another beer. He cracked it open, the echo riding out across the lake. I thought he might offer me a taste, for my birthday, but he kept it to himself.

We started toward the lighthouse.

*

Out on the lake, the mosquitoes were fewer. I watched my father steer. I wanted to ask him, Is the lighthouse really haunted?" But when the motor spewed to life, I couldn t hear anything. The sky became a deep, reddish blue.

Here," said my father, handing me a life jacket. The water gets rocky further out."

I set it aside—my father wasn t wearing one—but he insisted.

For your mother s sake," he said. He pointed toward the shore and watched me get buckled.

Our town became smaller farther out.

*

We rode through the darkness. Every so often, I could see the rippled lake in front of us, lit by the lighthouse. The motor cut off about ten yards from the island. The beach where we'd started was lost somewhere in the dark. I watched the giant tower as we approached, ancient and made of stone and reaching high into the sky, its light like a great North Star. No wonder no one could come here, I thought, staring at the black, crashing waves, at the wall of pointed rocks that encircled the island. I wasn't scared, exactly, because my father knew this place so well. But the world around us thundered. Was there about to be a storm? I wondered what my father would do next.

"We can drift the rest of the way," he said, wiping his lips on his arm and reaching for the rope.

I shivered, my feet icy, my clothes sticking to my skin. The waves knocked the boat up and down, the lake, normally still, having awakened near the lighthouse. It seemed like a different lake entirely.

I looked out at the shape of our town on the horizon, the shore where we'd stood and watched the lighthouse. I saw the shapes of houses, their tiny lights, but couldn't identify anything. It didn't even look like our town. I wondered if anyone could see us.

As I climbed onto the island, my father tied the boat against a post. The wind howled and blew my hair back and I couldn't hear anything over the loud wind and water. I wanted to tell him it was going to storm, that we probably shouldn't have come here tonight, but I knew I'd only be silenced by the gust. My father held my back and guided me along.

*

Inside the lighthouse, everything was black. The storm outside, or what sounded like a storm, got muffled by the lighthouse's heavy door. My father flipped a switch, and after a pause, flight by flight, the tower revealed itself. The interior of the lighthouse, with its tall, narrow staircase and gray stone design, resembled a castle, or maybe an old church–it was a place out of time. The smell of fish and mold was everywhere, reminding me of my father. When I looked at the window, stained yellow with age, I noticed a silverfish scurrying upward.

I figured we were going up, too. But he stopped me.

"Look," said my father. His voice echoed. He pointed to a panel on the wall.

"This is the brain of the lighthouse," he said. "The light at the top starts here. It runs all the way up, with wires. It gets changed all the time, this timer, because of the seasons, the way the days are always changing. Do you see it? This is what turns it on and off."

He fingered the buttons and wires. I wanted to get a closer look, but he was standing in front of it, blocking my view. He whispered to himself, seeming to be doing a mental checklist. It looked very old, the mechanisms in the box, but it was well taken care of. The wires were organized and neat. I turned to the window beside us, slatted with iron bars. A sludge hung down from the sill. A thick, caked material.

"Guano," said my father. "The birds like to rest there when it's open."

On the boat, I'd put on sandals, a pair of my father's, too big for my feet, but otherwise, all I had on were my jeans and a loose-fitting shirt. I shook in the cold.

"Remind me to wipe this down," said my father. He began to climb the stairs.

Because of the stink, I tried to hold my breath, but was soon exhausted. The stairs went on forever. My father climbed to the top without slowing. I was surprised at his energy. He must have been in good shape, beneath his long coat. At the top of the staircase, we came to another door. Outside, the lake wind moaned.

"Are we going back out?" I said.

"Of course," said my father.

Because of the wind, the door slammed back against the circular stone wall. We stepped out onto the thin porch at the top of the lighthouse.

The breeze above the lake was overwhelming. It forced us back against the building, wild and deafening, but my father walked over without fuss and leaned against the railing. He signaled me closer.

"Look at the water," he shouted.

The lake was dark black, galactic. Speckled with constellations, it blurred in the current, interrupted in patterns by the rotating light at the top of the lighthouse.

"It looks like it goes on forever," I said.

"It looks that way some nights," he told me. Then he said, "be careful." He pointed out another patch of guano.

The moon shone down on the rippled water, and at the top of the tower the wind felt alive. I squinted in the power of it, but my father kept on staring, unfazed.

"Do you see that blinking light, all the way out west?" he asked. "There's another lighthouse out that way."

I traced the point of my father's finger to the dim, blinking light. In the darkness, the far away light appeared lonesome. I leaned out over the ledge to see better, but my father pulled me back in.

"A man will drown getting that close to the edge."

I looked at my father in the shadows. His face seemed a mile away, lit in segments by the glowing lights inside. He stared out over our town, looking stern and serious. I shared his gaze. I began to feel dizzy. Again, I wondered what he was thinking, what he'd meant when he'd told me that nothing went on in our town without him seeing. It was hard to make out anything from this far off.

I leaned against the stone of the building. My father walked the deck, alone in the dense, moaning winds.

"Now you're one of only two folks in town who have seen it all," he yelled at me.

I braced myself in the strong, bitter cold. I wondered how long we would stay here, at the lighthouse. It would take a long time to get back home. I thought of my mother in the kitchen, worried and wondering what had happened to us. With my arms tucked into my shirt, I measured the shapeless water between the town and my father in his sanctuary. I tried to find my house across the lake.

# Sister Holly

At the far end of our street there is a cul-de-sac, a dead end of houses removed from the proper neighborhood. We gather in the woods behind the cul-de-sac, in a clubhouse built at the top of a tree, titled with an old bar sign one of us stole from the rubble of a nearby fire: *The Rusty Nail.*

From our clubhouse, we can see into the homes of the cul-de-sac. A pair of old hags own two of the properties, the ancient Agmon sisters, whose rundown houses face each other across the street. Other than to investigate the strange whirring noises that come from their bedrooms at night, we've had no reasons to study them.

The third house, painted pale yellow so that it stands out from the plain white others, and with large, uncurtained windows, belongs to Sister Holly. Sister Holly is the youngest nun we've ever seen—all of us students at the local Catholic boys' high school. She must be just a few years older than us, and she doesn't teach, as far as we know. Each day she leaves her house in full uniform, heading to an unknown place—a convent in the city, we imagine, or some other queer religious institute. Our parents call her *Sister Holly,* the italics a tone in their voices, when referencing her.

"Poor Lottie Miller," says my mother to my aunt one evening at the kitchen table. Across the room, my father sits in his usual chair, whittling a piece of wood into some sort of knick-knack. "That daughter of hers is gonna end up in the family way."

"A disciple of *Sister Holly,*" says my aunt.

Our street is full of these sayings, innuendos, though we've never seen anyone at the pale-yellow house but its owner. In the clubhouse, we share our findings, trying to understand the young nun.

"Ms. Marsh said she's had an abortion," says one of us.

"Who's Ms. Marsh?"

"She works at the clinic."

"You've never been to any clinic."

"She got expelled from the convent. That's why she can't teach here in town."

"I'd confess my sins to *Sister Holly* any day."

We swap binoculars in the evening, watching Sister Holly's routines on the top floor of her house. Her hair falls down to her shoulders, dark and slick from the shower. She wears a towel, or else a pair of underwear. She lies on her bed with a book, her feet in the air. We encourage her to go further. "Roll over!" we chant. We become obsessed with the word "abortion." She's the first and best woman any of us have ever seen; a curse printed in the Bible by mistake.

One day we're sitting in The Rusty Nail when one of us dares another to sneak into the pale-yellow house in the cul-de-sac. Of course, we've all thought it before. Sister Holly has a hold on us. The girls on our street, who attend our sister-high school, distract us during the day, but Sister Holly keeps us up at night. Those with girlfriends choose the sway of Sister Holly's legs, prefer her discolored white bras to the lacy black show bras of their girlfriends. The grotesque faces of the nuns at school only elevate our affection.

"What would be the point?" the dared boy asks. "She'd freak out and call the cops on us. She'd close her windows up for good."

"Then go in when she's out in the city, or wherever she goes all day."

"That would be even more pointless."

The mission, of course, is obvious. "Bring us back a souvenir."

But the nervous boy backs down. "It's not worth it. It'll ruin everything."

"It won't ruin nothing."

That's when I hear myself volunteer. The boys have been joking around, all of us packed in the clubhouse, sweating and bored in the late spring sun. They turn to see me—a slight, thin boy in the corner of the fort—to figure me out. It's not often I have their attention.

"I'm serious," I say. I take the binoculars and look inside the familiar window. "You can watch from up here."

The boys look around the clubhouse. "Well, what are you waiting for?"

"Tomorrow," I tell them. "After school."

We all know Sister Holly will be home at any minute.

*

At sundown, we leave the clubhouse and go home for dinner. I change my clothes to hide the cigarette smoke, which hangs like a fog around our tree. As we eat, my mother talks about her job at the Sunday school, my father grunts at the appropriate pauses. I drink two glasses of milk and sit beside him after dinner as he whittles what appears to be a small balsa rabbit.

In bed I can't sleep; my nerves feel electric. I replay the afternoon in my head–the wide, uncertain eyes of the boys–then picture again the pale yellow house. It has two stories, like ours, though the houses on our street are larger, constantly under construction–basements added, swimming pools dug–so the houses in the cul-de-sac appear old, from another time. I wonder about the inside of the house, the mysterious layout of the rooms. I close my eyes and take a deep breath. I try to see the décor of the hallway: modest and beige; crucifixes, lots of them, hanging at a tilt. I imagine the smell of her bathroom, her soap, the feel of her carpet on the soles of my feet. I think of her underwear, and then I'm really going.

The next day, I get to school early. I worry about the other boys, if they've taken me seriously. But they tease me in a brotherly way. They raise their hands in class, deflecting the inquiries of the nuns. The nuns act suspicious, slanting their eyes, but they carry on as usual. It amazes me that the girl in the cul-de-sac could be one of them, could have anything to do with these old, bitter women. In the back of the classrooms, I bite my lips and watch the clocks, wanting this day to go on forever.

Soon the final bell rings and on the way to the Rusty Nail the boys talk.

"She's a nympho," says one boy. "You're so lucky."

"In his dreams," they laugh.

A small boy, not usually one of us, has come along to the clubhouse today. Somebody's cousin.

"I wouldn't do it if I were you," says the cousin.

"Well, you're not him," I'm defended. I haven't had to speak all day.

They pass around the binoculars. I can't see her dresser, but it has to be nearby—in the corner of the bedroom, against the far wall, beside the window. We establish an emergency signal, in case Sister Holly returns ahead of schedule: the boys will fire a bright orange flare gun one of them stole from his father's safe box.

As an extra precaution, we check the soundless homes of the Agmon sisters. Nothing to report. I get punched and patted and have fingers run through my hair. I'm assured the binoculars will track my every move until I'm there, inside the house, and will wait for me at the bedroom window. I'm wished good luck and warned not to chicken out.

And then, I'm off, climbing down the clubhouse. My stomach turns as they chant my name and I cross the woods into the cul-de-sac, calculating my footsteps, careful not to trip. The sun feels hot on my neck and shoulders. I'm carrying the heavy weight of their eyes.

At the front of the house, I check the curve of the street—no one to catch me, to mistake me for a burglar—before taking the key from the potted plant beside the door. Everything is right. The lock of the pale yellow house submits, and I shut the door and the rest of the world behind me.

Finally, I exhale. The first thing I notice in the foyer is a smell, an earthy scent, like flowers steeping, an old newspaper turned yellow. A woman's scent, I imagine, though my mother has never smelled that way. In the dark of the hallway, I survey my surroundings, eager to report my findings. A small bronze mirror hangs beside the doorway, square and smudged, and a pair of shiny black church shoes waits patiently beside an empty umbrella bin. I pick up the shoes and examine their insides, worn and stiff, larger than I expected. I sniff them, on a whim. On a table nearby, a single framed photo of an unknown dog greets the entrance (whose dog? I wonder, looking around the house, hearing nothing), a smiling beast with a branch between its jaws.

Strange as it is, I don't see any religious memorabilia—no crucifix on the wall, no cozy embroidered prayers, like at my home. If her house is anything like mine, I think, I'll find the stairs in the next room over, beside the den, but instead, I'm somehow in the kitchen. Looking around, I picture the young nun, for the first time, eating: thin crisps and celery sticks, her teeth lightly crunching. The room seems well ordered, except for the sink, in which a tower of dirty dishes leans out over the counter. I wonder if the nun has recently cooked for someone, or if she's just a slob, though both seem hard to imagine. A teakettle sits on the stove, probably from breakfast. I want to investigate her refrigerator, but I decide against it when I come across the stairs.

I move slowly upward, but each step, with a creak, alerts the house of my presence. I know I'm alone, but the sound makes my heart race. The walls of the stairwell are bare, but I take my time in the darkness. I linger outside the bedroom, preparing to be rejoined with the boys.

With a deep breath, I turn the knob and enter the bedroom. I recognize it right away. It feels like someplace fictional come to life. It also seems smaller in person. Immediately, I go to the window and search for The Rusty Nail. To my surprise, I can't see the tree or the clubhouse from this angle. I'm somehow blocked by trees. I squint and wave to the invisible others; I put on a show, knowing that somewhere out there they're fighting for the binoculars. Remembering the way they'd treated me at school, I lie down on the bed in my sneakers, rolling into Sister Holly's position, basking in their excitement like a cat in the sun.

I return to the window and bid them farewell. Now I'm feeling better. The dresser waits across the room; I saunter over. Rifling through the drawers, I expect to find a neat supply of nuns' clothing—rows of squarely folded black and white outfits. Instead, I find sweatshirts, and in the next drawer down, some slacks and old jeans.

The final drawer contains the treasure. Chewing my tongue, I inspect it all: the textures and discolorations, the minor holes and stains. I finger the cotton fabrics; I pinch them between my fingers; I hold them up to my face. No one can see me alone in this bedroom. Without discrimination, I shove a pair of each kind in my pocket, wadding them up into tight, little balls. On impulse, I also take a pair of stockings and a second pair of underwear. These I shove into the waist of my pants for safe keeping.

With my mission complete, I make a reappearance in the window, holding up my souvenirs like flags. Between the branches, I think I can see the orange reflection of the flare gun waved in celebration. I wonder what the group will do with these findings, if Sister Holly will notice them gone.

Because I want to make the experience last, I decide to use the bathroom before I go. The pressure of the heist has sunken into my stomach, and, in a stroke of excited genius, I think of using the bathroom and not flushing—a calling card to leave behind, like the criminals on TV. I cross the room and click on the light of the master bathroom.

Then I freeze in place.

Sister Holly swings a large, white iron, steaming and plugged into the nearby outlet. She has on her nun's uniform, squatting barefoot on the tile beside the toilet.

"Get back," she warns.

I want to run, to scream, but I only just stand there and stare in her direction. She holds the iron out, short and trembling, and I don't know what to do. I've never seen her up close before, none of us have, and I look into her wide, brown eyes. She looks even younger in person; her face is small and alert and on her left cheek there is a scar in the shape of a triangle. She stares back, she can't seem to understand why I haven't moved. She whispers something again and again in stunted breaths, and I realize at this moment that I've never heard her voice before.

"What do you want?" she asks. "Why won't you leave?"

She tilts her head, looks at my waist, at the stain I've yet to notice. Slowly, she stands upright.

"Whatever you want," she says, speaking quietly, still gripping her weapon, "just hurry." The room smells like fire and I want her to take a swing. To make a move. But instead, the curling iron lowers to her side. She looks in my eyes.

That's when I finally run. I race down the stairs and out of the cul-de-sac. I don't run to the clubhouse, but back home, to my bedroom. I lock the door. I rip off my jeans, still hot and wet, and the damp underwear and stockings fall out limp on the floor. When I hear the pounds of the boys' hyper fists on my bedroom door, I kneel beside my bed, naked from the waist down, and cry.

# The River

If the river had a name, we never knew it. It was a muddy, winding river, our river. It travelled east to west across the state.

One day, at the start of summer, we got the idea to walk it, front to back.

It was *our* river, after all. We should see the whole thing. We heard it started in L—, the next town over. We set off at our usual part of the river and headed east. We brought along our fishing rods, Mikey's knife, and a roadmap I'd found in my dad's car. It didn't prove too helpful. We turned it over and over. Mikey got pissed and threw it in the river. We knew well enough how to survive.

"All we need to do is follow the river," said Mikey.

It was a long walk to L—, and we made the voyage barefoot, our feet socked in callus from all the time spent on the river. We stopped for a swim now and then when the sun was hot.

"I'm starving," said Mikey.

We fished.

Around here, on that part of the river, there weren't many trees around, so we fished in the wide-open sun.

"Goddamn," said Mikey. "We should've brought snacks."

"Hobos don't pack snacks," I said.

"It's hot as hell. The fish in L— don't know how to eat."

I didn't tell Mikey, but we hadn't left our town yet. The path to L– was a ten-mile hike.

When I finally snagged one, Mikey dropped his line. He held my shoulders and yanked to help me reel it.

"Don't fuck this up," he shouted. "I'm starving."

It was a good-sized mudfish, strong and brown, its mouth dripping mud. I laid it on the grass. Mikey went to work, slicing it open, splitting the meat. He was better than me at gutting. He said he didn't feel anything for a fish. "They don't have feelings," he said. He didn't either, said Mikey. The knife sunk in deep, releasing a gooey flatulence, a stream of blood. Mikey began to saw. He scooped out the innards and tossed them in the grass. The flies started buzzing.

"I'll get a fire going," I said.

"I'm too hungry."

"You mean eat it raw?"

"Like sushi, ain't it?"

I'd never had sushi before. I doubted Mikey had either.

He took a few hunks of meat and washed them in the river. He came back and divvied them up and took the first bite. He squirmed as he swallowed it down.

"Is it that bad?"

He spit. The spit was pink and mushy.

"It tastes like shit. No worse than when it's cooked, though. Here."

He gave me a piece and I ate it whole. It tasted like mud, rich and foul, like this fish had nothing but mud in its veins.

Suddenly, Mikey started howling.

"I'm feeling crazy," he said. "Something about eating it raw like that."

He howled again and hopped on one foot. He pulled down his trunks and for a second he stood there naked in the sun, screeching and stamping in the dirt.

I howled, too. I could feel it, the muddy metallic taste on my tongue, worming around in my belly. When Mikey jumped in the river, I followed suit.

"It's like we're part fish now or something," he said.

We swam for a while, our arms and legs splashing. The water was warm and cloudy.

We got out and rested. I didn't want to say it, but my stomach was starting to churn. We kept on for another few minutes and then stopped. Mikey puked in the river. His puke was thick and red. We watched it flow downstream.

We didn't make it to L— that day.

The next weekend, my dad drove us out east. We stomped through the woods, me and Mikey, hunting for the start of our river. Our tracking skills were good in our own woods, but here our senses were strained. It was familiar, but with a different sort of feel than our woods, a different smell and way about it.

"I don't see any river," said Mikey.

My dad was the one who found it. He called us over.

It was a small, mossy hole in the ground, no bigger than a snake's nest, in a dark patch of woods just off trail. We had to brush some leaves to see it. A little stream came trickling out, flowing westward in a narrow, muddy trench.

"No way," said Mikey. "That can't be it."

"Sure, it is," said my dad. "It probably goes on a ways underground. But this is where it starts on land."

Mikey jumped into the trench.

"Careful," said my dad.

He inspected the hole on all fours.

"You're saying if I plug it up right here, I could stop it forever, like right fucking now?"

"Language," said my dad. "It's possible. Of course, if it rains it'll probably start up again. At least for a while. It's hard to know for sure."

Mikey kicked some dirt into the hole.

"Quit!" I said.

"Shut up," said Mikey. The water was still flowing. "You think I want to dry it up? It's our damn river. But damn, it's hard to believe."

*

Another time we headed west to the other end of the river.

The western ending point was Lake Michigan, one of the five Great Lakes. Along the way, it twisted and widened. It started in L— and travelled through our town, then to another county out west, then, eventually, it emptied in the big blue lake. We pictured the brown, sludgy water from our river mixing with the nice, blue waves. Probably it made a nasty foam. It was about a thirty mile walk in that direction. We weren't going to make it on foot, but we started anyway. It was a hot day. We brought along peanuts for protein. We made it as far as we could, which was the start of the cornfields and farmland two miles upriver. We stopped to rest and in doing so we met some girls. There were three of them, each about our age, with freckles and pale skin. They were swimming in the river, in a spot where the river widened and people would swim, while a woman who was probably their mom watched from the grass nearby. Mikey called to them as we came over.

"I don't want to," I said.

"Come on, dude, it's girls."

"We're not even a quarter of the way yet."

"Who cares? It's just a dumb river."

The girls had matching bathing suits that were colorful and tight. They looked like fish or mermaids. Mikey was loud and swore a lot. The girls watched him and laughed. He did handstands in the river and cartwheels in the grass. He splashed the girls, who yelled but laughed and splashed him too. He asked them, all three of them, "Is your mom going to leave soon?" and when the girls shook their heads and said "why?" he said something dirty, which shocked them. He looked at the mom after and waved, but the mom didn't wave back. The whole time Mikey was doing it, I stood in the river too, behind him, following his lead and laughing along with the girls, as if I were just as charmed by Mikey as they were.

When the mom called the girls in to leave, we stayed in the river. One of the girls had a wedgie when she got out and Mikey pointed. The girl flicked the rubbery suit with a gentle snap and Mikey started laughing.

When they were out of range, he said to me, "You couldn't see it, but one of them let me touch her underwater."

"No, she didn't."

"Yeah, she did."

"Which one?"

"The hot one."

"They all looked the same."

"No, they didn't."

"Touch where?"

"You know where."

"Inside her bathing suit?"

"All the way in."

"When?"

"Like, just a few minutes ago, before they got out."

I thought it over.

"Wouldn't a bunch of water get in?" I said.

He laughed. "Goddamn, you're dumb."

I shoved him underwater.

"You weren't even talking," he said.

"Yeah, I was."

"Well, talking's not what I did."

"If you say so."

"Right in front of their mom."

"Was it really their mom?"

"Who cares?"

We climbed out and dried in the sun. We headed east. We were tired and hungry and we knew we wouldn't reach the far end of the river today. We ate the peanuts which made us thirsty, and we drank from the muddy river and hiked back to our part of the river and went to sleep.

# Second Bride

Roger proposed to Madeline, but not on bended knee. They held the wedding in the assisted living home parlor. They served a buffet meal. Residents came, on foot or wheeled in from their portable beds, intermixed with nurses, visiting families, unwitting guests. The staff played old Elvis CDs from the parlor room speakers. Madeline's sons took photos of the decorations, the wedding dress, the kiss.

My mother and I stood in the back of the parlor, watching my grandfather and his wife. We'd been there since the start of the party, not eating or drinking or joining in the fun.

"She's not your grandmother," said my mom, "who was a saint for putting up with him." My eyes were on the cake at the side of the parlor. I'd never been to a wedding before. My mother said, "he's making a fool out of her," and I thought she meant Madeline, who in that moment was slow dancing with my grandfather to "Loving You," both of them hardly moving, but looking happy, my grandfather more alert than usual, in a long blue suit, and I was confused and angry at her, my unromantic mother, for trying to spoil the day.

# Naomi

"Naomi Leigh White," said my mother. We were playing cards at the table again. Outside, the rain made a pool in the hill of our backyard.

"How come *Leigh*?" I asked.

I'd heard the answer before, but I liked to hear stories more than once. She looked at me and I added, "Go fish."

"Leigh was your grandmother's name," she said.

"I thought her name was Jeanie?"

"That was your other grandma." She took a long sip from her mug, blowing on the steam, and I took one from mine.

"How about fives?" I asked.

"Go fish."

I drew my cards and studied them, or at least pretended to.

"What's so special about Grandma Leigh?" I asked. "Why not Naomi Jeanie White?"

"Nothing special about Leigh," said my mother. "But definitely better than 'Naomi *Jeanie* White'."

"Naomi Jeanie White," I repeated.

"Do you have any jacks?"

"Go fish. Was Grandma Leigh *your* mom or Dad's?"

"You know she was mine."

"I know," I said.

"Well, don't ask questions when you already know the answer."

I looked at the rain outside. It was building against the sliding glass door.

"Where do the squirrels go when it rains?"

"In their trees," said my mother.

"I knew that, too. They live inside the holes. But don't they still get wet?"

"Have you ever seen a wet squirrel?" she asked. Both of us laughed a little, picturing it. "Your turn."

"Hmm, do you have any sixes?"

She gave me one card. I waved my arms to bother her, because I knew she doesn't like to lose.

"How old was I when Grandma Leigh died?" I asked.

"You were two."

"How old am I now?"

"You know I'm not going to answer that. Do you have any kings?"

"Go fish," I said. "How old would she be today?"

She stopped to think. "Seventy-one."

"No," I said. "Naomi Jeanie White."

"Naomi *Leigh* White," she corrected me.

"Naomi *Leigh* White."

"She would have been eighteen months in September," said my mother.

"That's still a baby."

"*You're* still a baby. Now take your turn."

I sat up, wanting to say I wasn't, but just then my father came home. He burst in the door and stamped his wet boots. He made a lot of squeaking noise, so I covered my ears. My mother gave me a look that meant stop talking.

"Hi Malcolm," said my mother when he entered.

My father grunted. He smelled like the lake because he worked at the lighthouse, and when it rained he had to make extra sure the lighthouse kept working.

"Raining like hell," says my father.

"Language," said my mother. "Take off your shoes." He went to the kitchen for a beer.

"Spotlight's flickering. Loose wire. I've got it now, but it won't last."

"I'll fix it," I said.

"Hush," said my mother.

"You can't even tie your shoes," said my father.

"Can too," I said.

I reached down to show him, but my feet were bare. My mother stopped me before I could run off to find them.

"Take your turn," she said.

"What are you doing?" asked my father.

"What else?"

"Do you have any kings?" I said.

My mother gave me two, then paused.

"Hold on, I asked for kings on my last turn. I'm not going to play with a cheater."

"I didn't hear you," I said.

My father stood behind me. I could feel his cold wetness on my back without him touching.

"Give me your kings," said my mother. Both she and my father were staring now. I folded my arms and waited until my father changed the subject.

"Lunch?" he said.

My mother put her cards down.

"There's lasagna in the fridge."

"*Lee*-sagna," I said.

My mother glared. I didn't like to be called a cheater.

"Have you ever seen a wet squirrel before?" I said to my father.

"Don't think so. They're too smart to get wet. Not like me." He took a drink from his beer.

I took one from my mug. The cocoa had cooled to a grainy chocolate milk. "Not like me," I sang. "Not-like-me. Na-o-mi."

"Stop it," said my mother. "What's gotten into you?"

"I'm not a cheater!" I shouted.

I ran to get my shoes and show them I could tie them, but when I got back to the table, my father had gone. I picked up my cards, but my mother wasn't watching. She was staring at the endless rain. I fiddled with my shoes under the table. I could hear my father down the hall, his boots still squeaking. I wanted to go outside.

Then he exploded.

"Goddamn fucking hell," he shouted.

"Is it out?" said my mother.

He slammed the door behind him. Everything shook.

I looked at my mother, who didn't say "language" this time. I thought about those words. I repeated them in my head. They stuck around in the kitchen long after my father had gone—cold, fishy words, like the way my father smelled.

"Come on," I said. "Keep playing."

My mother still wouldn't look at me. I said it again, no answer.

"Come on, are you broken?"

She sat there and watched the mounting rain.

"I hate it here," I said.

I got up and ran to the door. With a heavy pull, the water crashed

against me, all the rain that had built against the house. I slipped and cracked my head on the tile. My mother yelled as the rain poured over me, cold and metallic. I thought for a second I might drown.

# Mudfish

A mudfish is a kind of trout that lives in muddy rivers. The meat of a mudfish is muddy and tough. We caught a ton of mudfish in our river, but we always let them go. A mudfish doesn't eat mud, exactly, but it tastes like they eat mud for breakfast, lunch and dinner.

Mudfish are ugly, too. Most of the mudfish in our river were scarred and scabbed from already being caught before. My dad said, "It's how you know that mudfish are stupid." It was the first thing he ever said to me I knew was wrong.

To Mikey and me, a mudfish was good at surviving. The slices on their face made them look prehistoric, like they'd lived in our river for millions of years. Anything around that long had to be smart. That's what me and Mikey thought. If not smart, at least good at surviving.

We called ourselves mudfish because we too were good at surviving. We knew our way around the woods and river. We started fires and left secret markers in the trees to get around.

One day, Mikey said, "I got an idea."

We were standing by the river. We'd both caught ourselves a mudfish. They were laying in the sun.

Mikey took his knife out and picked up one of the mudfish. Instead of cutting it from its gills to its tailfin, he chopped the head clean off. That wasn't his usual way. He was having some fun. He picked up the head and held it in the air like a prize. He tossed it up and caught it and then kissed it on the lips. He laughed and chucked it back in the river. The mudfish's head floated upriver, toward the lake.

Next, he picked up the headless body from the grass. "This here is a damn good mudfish," he said.

"That one's mine," I told him.

"So what? You want to go first?"

"I'm not hungry," I said.

"Me either."

Mikey had a funny look in his eyes. He made that face sometimes, like when he was talking to girls, or doing something crazy.

Without saying anything, he pulled down his trunks. Sometimes we got naked in the river; it wasn't such a big deal. It was fun to feel free in the river. Mikey spent more time naked that than I did. He had a bunch of hair on his body and liked to show it off. After swimming and drying in the sun, I usually put my trunks back on, but Mikey liked to keep his off. He leapt in the grass and had a good time. His penis bounced up and down like a bobblehead and he thought it was funny.

Standing there naked, he stuck a finger into the fish, where the head had used to be. It made a gushy sound. He scraped around and pulled out the guts, tossing the slop and bones into the river. He put his finger back into the fish.

"Feels like the real thing," he laughed.

He ran his finger on the rim of the fish, stretching it out and saying, "You want a turn?"

"A turn at what?"

He lowered the fish. The sun was bright and burning. I turned away and stared at the other fish on the ground, Mikey's catch. It breathed a little, or tried to. It was a tiny mudfish. I held my breath to imitate its gasping.

When I turned back, Mikey was done with the fish. His skin was slick and red. He wiped himself off and tossed the empty mudfish back into the river. He put on his trunks and picked up the other fish. This time, he cut the belly first. He pulled the knife from the gills to the tail. He cleaned the fish and left its lifeless body on the grass. He closed his knife and walked upriver.

I stood there by the dead fish in the grass. Mikey was getting farther away, so I jumped in the river and swam to him. The current was strong and muddy and cool.

When I reached him, I climbed out of the river. Mikey was sitting on the grass.

"I forgot to say," he said, "I won't be here tomorrow. I have to go to my grandma's."

"Hobos don't have grandmas," I said.

"Sure, they do."

"Well, mudfish don't."

"What the hell are you talking about? Everyone's got a grandma. Don't be an idiot."

The sun got closer to the water. Some days we thought it might fall in. We didn't talk much by the river. I thought about the fish on the grass and the head in the river.

The next day, I went back to the same part of the river. I wanted to see if the gutted fish was there, where we'd left it. But it wasn't. Or at least I couldn't find it. Mikey was there, though.

"I thought you said you weren't coming," I said.

"Where else would I be?"

We sat around the river and fished. We cooked in the late summer sun.

# On the Night of the Party

They had gone to the party and left soon after, not wanting to make a big scene. Because he had driven, she left on foot, walking without direction and finding herself in a nearby park—or really a field beside a hill with no benches. Beneath the cold, starless night, he followed. They sat together on a pair of abandoned cinderblocks, which seemed to sprout up from the ground.

"It won't be so bad," said Charlie. "And not for so long. You don't have to worry."

She twisted her neck, long and goose-bumped in her cocktail dress.

"How can I not worry?" said Becka. "What kind of person would I be?"

"It's a support position, that's all. They wouldn't take me for the real stuff if I tried, not now."

From a block away, they could hear the party, an elaborate get-together for a friend who'd been promoted to some high company position.

"We can write letters," he went on, "like in the old days, remember? It might even be romantic. We'll be like young lovers, across the sea."

"*Like* young lovers?" she said. "What exactly are we, then?"

"I'm not so young."

"I'm going to be sick."

"Just calm down."

She looked ahead at the darkness on the hill. He stared at his feet.

"We've both had a little to drink tonight."

"Not enough," said Becka.

"I'll agree with you there."

"*You'll agree with me there*. You try to act so cute when we're fighting."

"Give me a break."

"What do you want me to say? Did you really expect me to be happy? Do you even remember the old days? Honestly, I don't know which I prefer, the jealous boy who hit me between tours or the man who makes cute jokes to make things better."

They sat in the empty park and listened to the party. It sounded like a lively time. A mosquito landed on one of Charlie's shoes and he watched it try to suck.

"You know I'm not like that," he said. "It was just the one time."

"If you say so," said Becka.

She combed her fingers through her hair. Every so often, there seemed to be someone in the darkness, on top of the hill, but it might have been a trick of her eyes.

"Of course, I say so," said Charlie. "It was a long, long time ago. We were kids."

"But you miss those days. That's the point. Most men your age would take a pill. But you're going overseas. And you have no good way of telling me. You don't sit us down so we can have an adult discussion. You try to be cute, and you show me like *this*."

She pointed to his head, recently shaved, and trembling in the cold night. He'd left his hat at the party.

"I thought it might be good this way," he said. "Not so serious. Besides, you used to like me this way."

She ignored him.

"It's perfectly safe," he went on. "I'll just be consulting. It's not like before. It's a big, air-conditioned building. There's no danger."

"In the desert. Don't leave out that part."

"I'll be fine."

"You'll be halfway across the world."

"I'll be safe."

"Stop saying that."

"Start hearing me," he said.

She turned to hide her face so he wouldn't see.

"You need to move away from me," she said.

Charlie got up and left the park. He walked down the sidewalk, not toward the party, but down the opposite block. The night was quiet further out. He bit his lip in the cold. He looked at all the houses, so big in this part of the city—absurdly big—but warm with lights.

After all this time, he thought, she could still be like this.

It was dumb to do it this way, he thought, on the night of the party. It hadn't been the safety net he'd planned.

It was a glorified desk job. Though he'd stopped short of calling it that to Becka.

He turned at the end of the block, and when he did, the giant houses started to shrink some. He felt a little better here, less claustrophobic. He hated to go to this part of the city. Becka loved it. To him, it didn't make sense—she hadn't budged an inch when he'd mentioned the money. She should've been ecstatic.

He kept on until he came to a drug store at the end of the street. He went in, and from the bottom shelf, he grabbed a fifth of brandy.

Back outside, he drank beneath the stars. It was all the same sky, wasn't it? He needed to explain it to Becka. He would make her understand.

When he returned to the park, he sat down by Becka. She hadn't moved from the cinderblock. He took a swig from the bottle, and before he could offer, she took it from his hands. For a while, they drank in silence, in the echo of the party.

"I guess they're fine without us," said Charlie.

"It's beautiful here, isn't it?" said Becka.

"Yes," he said. "It's nice."

She leaned against his shoulder.

"I've been watching this hill for a while," she said. "I think there's someone on there."

"Where?"

She pointed into the darkness. The night was alive before them, constantly shifting.

"It's probably just some pervert," he said.

She laughed. "Some soldier. Leaving me alone with a pervert on a hill."

"I don't see anyone."

"Me either," said Becka. It was true; the shape was gone now. "You must have scared him off."

# Montjuic

Robert Montano witnessed the death of the young Tomas Ruiz at the Palazzo del Montjuic in Barcelona. The palazzo stood at the top of a hill, surrounded by antique cannons (decades since fired, pale and graffitied with peace signs, initials), and looked out over the city from the sky.

Montano had been drinking in the corner and reading from a copy of an old American novel, which he was working to translate into Catalan. It was a warm day in Spain, and though Montano had hidden himself in the shade of the palazzo, the main space in front of him—filled with running children, a young schoolteacher trying to command attention—was bright with sun, the ground-stones a thick sunlit yellow at his feet.

From his seat in the palazzo, Montano observed the crowd. One child in particular stood out to him—a girl with bold attributes, pinned hair. She wore white shorts that glowed against her skin, chasing a boy to the roof of the palazzo.

The teacher, moving to a table nearby, smiled at Montano. She was youthful in her own way, if no comparison to the children, with their bouncing limbs and hairless bodies. This seemed obvious to them both. She called to the children to settle. Lunch would soon end, and they would return to their lesson. Montano watched the girl in white shorts as she chased the boy overhead. He listened for the stamping of her feet.

The wine the old translator drank while he translated was dark, nearly black, a powerful Tempranillo. He consumed it often, and so the taste was smooth to him. He enjoyed the drinking and occasionally returned to his book. The Palazzo del Montjuic was not a quiet place in late summer, but Montano found comfort in the life all around him.

He watched the teacher reach for a cigarette, light it after several attempts, and puff in the sunlight. It perfumed the air. He could almost taste it, the smoke in her lungs, rising inside her like a slowly opening hand. Robert had given it up years ago, but the sight of a young woman smoking brought him pleasure. There are fewer concerns when you are younger. Turning the page, though he hadn't read to the end of it (he hadn't even brought a pencil for notation), he breathed the teacher's exhalation. He looked at the girl in white shorts. She was probably twelve or thirteen of age. He wondered if she'd ever smoked a cigarette. Montano had swiped his first at only ten.

He set down the book. His copy of the novel was worn, its spine holding onto the pages without conviction. At sixty-three, the translator felt his own body weakening, losing its grip. The novel, its author's last completion, was a personal treasure of Montano's, though it had never received much critical attention. No one had paid him for, or encouraged, his translation, but he'd imagined the challenge of this particular piece for years. It was not a linguistically difficult translation— it had been worked into Spanish some time before—but one that required dignity and respect.

The children continued eating, cursing, racing through the palazzo. Montano felt tired in the shade and looked for the girl in white shorts. A group of tourists had entered the palazzo; he could not see around them. They stood in a pack, a wide range of ages, trying to act respectful. Montano thought briefly of the history of the fortress, what he had read on the plaques on the stone walls, had heard from errant portions of the tours. But when he found the girl again, it no longer mattered. She was running, still on the roof of the palazzo, across the way, with the boy in front of her. He remembered a girl from his childhood, long forgotten. The young, nameless beauties in Montano's life amazed him.

"*No corrent,*" announced the teacher below. She peered around the tourists, who had stopped in the center of the palazzo and were listening to the guide. The sun made the teacher squint and purse her lips. This bothered Montano. He adjusted his seat in the shade of the palazzo. With his eyes closed, he listened to the shouting children, the grasping voice of the tour guide, the mixture of languages, the pulse of his own heart. Inside his eyelids, he saw the color red with all its intensity.

When he opened his eyes again, sometime later, he felt a pain from the sunlight. It had reached its highest point in the sky now, and peered into his corner, invading his space. As his eyes adjusted to the sunlight, the young Tomas Ruiz came down, like a bomb, onto the courtyard. The sound was startling, both soft and loud. It was disorienting, seeming to come later than the sight.

As Tomas fell, the translator became aware of two facts at once: first, that this boy (the name Tomas Ruiz would not be in the newspaper until the next morning) was going to be killed from the impact. And second, that the entire palazzo was going to see him die.

He could not have done anything to stop it from happening. He was an old man, and in any case, he was sitting too far away. When the boy reached the stone, Montano jumped and spilled wine on the ground, staining the tiles. A moment later, Tomas was surrounded. People were screaming and hiding their eyes. From his corner in the shadows, Montano followed the attention of the crowd, the panicked children, the frightened tourists. Then, looking up at the rooftop, he saw her on the edge of the palazzo, the girl in the shorts who had caught his attention, who had reminded him of something special. He watched her standing at the edge of the roof, her arms hanging loosely at her side. She was alone, looking down at the boy who had chased her. Because her hair was pinned, it did not blow in the wind like the flags behind her. He wanted to run to her. To take her away.

But this was not a possibility for Montano. He got to his feet and left the palazzo before the *policia* arrived. His book in hand, but the wine bottle behind him, he hurried down the road back to the city. From time to time, he looked behind him, to see if anyone was following. But of course, no one was. Robert Montano had done nothing wrong.

# Acknowledgements

"Homeless" in *The Axe Factory* (Spring 2016)

"A Story About Rain" and "Montjuic" in West Trade Review (Spring 2016, vol. 7)

"Safari" in *The Axe Factory* (Fall 2017)

"Under the Pier" in *Red Savina Review* (Spring 2016)

"Tick" in *Apple Valley Review* (Fall 2021)

"Kids" in *34th Parallel* (Winter 2021, #91)

"The Escapist" and "Second Bride" in *The Nomadic Journal: Sate* (February 2016)

"The Lighthouse Keeper" in The Bangalore Review (June 2015)

"Sister Holly" in *The Furious Gazelle* (June 2015)

"Naomi" in *fields* (Issue 5, February 2016)

"On the Night of the Party" in *Buck Off Magazine* (Spring 2016, vol. 5)

# About the Author

Alex Haber is a writer from Michigan. His stories have been published in West Trade Review, The Nomadic Journal, Buck Off Magazine, and others. His book *The Lighthouse Keeper* was published by Gnashing Teeth Publishing. He holds an MFA from George Mason University.